About

Nicola J John is a native of the fishing port of Aberaeron, west Wales. Educated at the local comprehensive school, she went on to gain an honours degree in science and education at University College, Cardiff, followed by a post graduate qualification in public and media relations.

Thereafter, she taught at several primary schools before setting up her own consultancy business and involvement with the National Lottery (Wales) and Welsh Water (Dŵr Cymru).

From an early age and with a love of Enid Blyton's book, *The Magic Faraway Tree,* and inspired by her late grandmother, she long harboured a secret desire to one day write something memorable herself.

Freed from the shackles of motherhood, and inspired by her husband's twin brother and his obsession with weeds despoiling his beautifully manicured lawns, she finally put pen to paper. The result lies within these pages.

She has two daughters, Bethan and Lucy.

Author photo credit: John Briggs

THE WEED MAN

NICOLA J JOHN

THE WEED MAN

Vanguard Press

VANGUARD PAPERBACK

© Copyright 2021
Nicola J John

A CIP catalogue record for this title is
available from the British Library.

ISBN 978 1 80016 086 6

Vanguard Press is an imprint of
Pegasus Elliot MacKenzie Publishers Ltd.
www.pegasuspublishers.com

First Published in 2021

Vanguard Press
Sheraton House Castle Park
Cambridge England

Printed & Bound in Great Britain

Dedication

To my loving and supportive husband who has
stood by me and broadened my horizons;
and to Charles James Sweet, 4th October 1955 to
5th July 2021.

Professor Gethin David Weedall woke following a very relaxing and peaceful night's sleep, his alarm clock reassuringly on time at six thirty a.m. Being a creature of habit, he was always up at the crack of dawn. He jumped out of bed feeling as bright as a button and full of energy.

"Well let's get ready for the mission possible," he would say.

His loving, long-suffering wife, Sally Anne, slumbered on contentedly. Or so Gethin thought. She was all too familiar with her husband's early morning ritual, and was not amused. His long-term aim was to create and establish the perfect grass lawn that could be admired by all.

In addition, he needed to win the hearts and minds of his fellow gardeners and earn their respect for his overzealous endeavours.

I need to do something outstanding, original and unique, he thought.

All I ask is that he'd stay in bed and pay a bit of loving attention to me from time to time. Instead, I have to compete with the other love in his life. I feel as if there are three dynamics within our marriage. Me, Gethin and his ever-nuisance *weeds*. Sally Anne felt frustrated and neglected as she hid snugly under their sumptuous duvet. However, she let her mind wonder.

She had a very vivid imagination and could easily drift into a parallel universe. This morning she was on Richard Branson's island of Necker, where she lay on the sun-kissed white sands wearing a very skimpy red bikini, sipping a pina colada and dreaming of her virtual lover. No names to be mentioned. However, she did have a thing about Lionardo De Capriot. (What a silly name.)

Meanwhile, back in the real world her husband was ready and eager to face the daily challenge ahead. He was beginning to enjoy his rather humble existence and less complicated way of life.

At last, I can appreciate the simple things in life. Having spent my career being pandered to and waited on had its advantages. However, this is my real world now. A loving wife, children and back to nature, fresh air along with the elements, he told himself.

Early retirement had presented the prof with some obstacles, both mentally and physically, which he was determined to overcome through self-therapy. He had thrown himself into his new hobby. *Weeding, weeding* and more *weeding*.

He was enjoying every minute of it. A bizarre pursuit you might think, though he was content with his on-going quest to fight his new-found deadly enemies, a mission far removed from his previous past working life.

"Those fresh-faced daisies and smiling yellow dandelions, along with the purple clover and blue forget-me-nots have simply got to go. Exterminated. For good!" the prof declared emphatically.

Well, that's what he believed in his slightly distorted outlook on life. For, oddly enough, his past would come back to haunt him in a strange and unexpected way.

"Oh! What a beautiful day for the killing field," he quietly said to himself with an air of self-importance and excitement. I'm going to have another productive session today. Action stations. Then it's lift off, he convinced himself.

The past is in the past, he kept telling himself unwittingly. How wrong this would prove to be.

He washed, and regimentally put on his favourite gardening gear, including his much-loved skimpy shorts emblazoned with prickly cacti, complemented by the essential green wellington boots, all his best friends and partners in his dastardly crime.

"Right. Weeding uniform in check. I'm ready and it's time to go." He smiled knowingly at the task ahead of him, the daily ritual he simply had to complete, if only to retain his own sanity. Well, he didn't want to admit to himself, or indeed his dear Mrs W, that he was beginning to lose the plot.

What a shame for someone so highly intelligent. He had a very brief moment of contemplation and reminiscence. He didn't look back in anger. Oh no! He knew well he was highly admired and respected by his fellow comrades within the secret service regime.

However, he missed being one of Her Majesty's Government's agents. His fight for world peace against political antagonism was over.

Since he'd retired, he was following a very different path. He was now having to face the inevitable mission impossible alone. No other battalion support.

Dressed in battle kit, he marched defiantly towards the enemy. With military precision he surveyed all before him. Then began slowly walking up and down the lawn, not missing a single blade of grass. Suddenly he spotted danger. A weed just ahead. A nasty weed. He took out his extra-large magnifying glass, bent down and scrutinised the foe. "Aha," he exclaimed. Yes. Definitely. It had to be exterminated.

He aimed his *Devitas* gun at the helpless growth spraying it and showing no mercy whatsoever as it heaved one last breath and keeled over, limp and beaten. Oh! What satisfaction the prof felt. For the next two hours he continued on his relentless mission.

Strange to think that it hadn't occurred to him to simply and easily pluck the weeds from the ground with his fingertips. But that would have been far too easy for a man of his stature. A man who believed in chemical warfare. And vengeance without scruples. Such was his former government training.

Well, in fact that was all about to change as he was soon to discover two new friends who would completely redirect his life in a very positive way.

This morning was no different to any other. But was it?

Having settled back into the mundane world of suburbia he was enjoying the peace and tranquillity of his own territory, his family garden. The pace of life was much slower than he'd been used to, as he was now faced with very different challenges. He'd been through a metamorphosis since returning from duty.

Life would never be quite the same again. He'd suffered-shell shock, amongst other conditions. However, he was on a positive rehabilitation process supported by his good, loving and ever-patient lady, along with his family.

Their long-standing family GP, Dr Richard Gardiner, had gently recommended taking up a pastime that would help Gethin focus on the future.

"I suggest you take up a new interest, Gethin. Something completely different. A hobby that you can throw all your energies into. Try to forget the past and focus on your beautiful wife and the children. Do something you can completely absorb yourself in and be proud of," the GP said.

Well, talking of food for thought, Gethin most certainly did.

Prof Gethin Weedall was not an individual to do anything by half measures. It was all or nothing. There was no middle ground. He took Dr Gardiner's advice very seriously.

He went to bed that night and woke up with the idea of: wait for it…

Weeding. Yes, that's right. Unusual, certainly. But true nevertheless and extreme.

On his next check-up at the doctor's surgery, he shared his excitement with his GP.

"Well, Prof Gethin, this does sound rather interesting. It's a new one on me. Are you sure about this? Being in the garden all day having to cope with our unpredictable weather throughout the four seasons?" he questioned with raised eyebrows.

"Well, there's only one way to find out, Doctor. I'm determined to give it my best shot, pardon the pun. Trust me, I am no quitter. As you of all people should know," he said, confidently.

In a short space of time he'd established himself as the *Serial Weed Killer of the North — and a highly respected pillar of the community.*

The weeding expert, as he became known, was on a very important project that morning. His ambition was to eliminate all unwanted foliage from his perfectly manicured front and back grass lawns.

He entered his somewhat cluttered garage to prise out his squeaky-clean and much-loved tools of the trade, including his bespoke industrial lawn mower and, most importantly, his precious green, quilted gardening gloves.

While perusing the contents before him he made a shocking discovery. He found his vital supply of the most powerful and deadly weedkiller was almost depleted. A mere day's supply left, at best. He rushed back to the house and poured his heart out. Poor Sally Anne, she was far from impressed and totally unsympathetic.

"Here we go again." She was all too used to his obsessive behaviour.

"My dear love," he said, hands trembling uncontrollably. "I've got some shocking news I must share with you," he said, waving his arms around dramatically. "We're all but out of *Devitas*. You know, my regular weedkiller. What on earth are we going to do? We can't let those evil green pests take over and ruin our perfectly kept garden," he almost pleaded, his face ashen, and as white as a sheet.

Mrs W looked at him with such devotion and a slight ache in her heart. After all, she had tried to be a caring and supportive wife. However, she was beginning to fear for her own sanity. Her loving husband of over four decades was beginning to try her patience. She had been his rock throughout this period of OCD with weeds. She felt neglected, a spare part that only served a purpose in a domestic capacity. Sadly, nothing more. Perhaps if she had dressed up in an all-green outfit now and again it might have caught his interest?

Oh. How she yearned for him to make a small gesture to show his appreciation. Just inviting her out for a drink and a small pub lunch, just now and again. Even a picnic by the nearby river, as they did when they were courting all those years ago.

This would have been more than welcome. Whilst going about her usual chores, she started reminiscing about their raunchy romps behind the bushes. The memories came flooding back like a tsunami. She was beginning to get a little carried away as her imagination took over.

Her feminine feelings were coming to life again and she started fantasising about making love, naked, with Professor GW on the front lawn. Secretly, she hoped their uninhibited behaviour would be the envy of their extremely conservative and boring neighbours.

I must stop having these colourful and graphic thoughts at my time of life. Is it normal to feel so sexy at 60? she asked herself. I keep remembering that film with Glenda Jackson and the alcoholic actor Oliver Reed. What was the name of it? *Women in love*, I think. It was wonderful, she reminisced aching for almost forgotten physical pleasures.

Perhaps I should make an effort to seduce my husband again with a romantic meal. A candle-lit supper accompanied with lots of good quality wine, prepared with love and of course the assistance and essence of that ever-loveable TV character Hyacinth Bucket, she pondered.

She laughed out loud at the very thought. She was on Fantasy Island again. Well, it made her smile to think about dragging him away from his ever-so-precious *weeds*.

On a more serious note, she thought: this could be the answer to our prayers. To her the professor was away somewhere in cloud-cuckoo-land as usual whilst she was stuck at home contemplating her role in life. She wasn't depressed exactly. Just feeling a little low and sombre from time to time.

Surely, I must be more alluring than those green prickly pests? she repeatedly asked herself, self-doubt flooding through her normally resolute persona.

She took a brief look at herself in the mirror and thought: Hang on, I've given birth twice, had a number of lady procedures and I feel as if I'm still a teenager. Why can't my husband recognise this? I've never been into one of those take away or convenient restaurants and always tried to look after myself.

Call me a snob but I am very proud that I have always cooked at home and painstakingly looked after Gethin and all the family with my culinary delights. Whilst at food college, I was awarded a special prize for creating a new product for Sainsbury's. I got on radio Wales and given a fifty pound voucher. I felt like I had won the Lottery.

Well, I was a mere student at the time and the small fame and fortune meant a great deal to me then.

So many fragments of their lives changed after they married. A wonderful wedding with no expense spared to make it a momentous and special occasion. A special day filled with music and dancing aplenty. Inevitably after all the build up to the ceremony it was back to earth.

The children quickly came along and suddenly life became a different planet. A seemingly less loving world on a personal and intimate level. Sally Anne missed Gethin's amorous affection and that precious sense of belonging so much. However, she also enjoyed being a mum. What fun.

However, their daughters, Judith and Mary, were now grown up. Healthy and happy! They had both fled the nest and had families of their own to care for. Sally Anne missed them so much. Suddenly there was a vacuum, and a big void in her life. She yearned to find something to refill her life. She contemplated flower arranging at the church and getting involved with the local school sports association. Well, after all, she was an Olympic shot putter, a silver medallist, something to be proud of.

No. She became a little negative thinking. This is my bed and I must lie in it.

I suppose this is a normal way of life for us now, she sighed. Or did it have to be so. Surely this should be *our* time? I've given Gethin the best part of my life and it would be good to feel loved and needed again, she was feeling slightly melancholy but with no bitterness or anger.

Stand by your Man, she kept telling herself in the words of the iconic singer, Dolly Parton.

"Well, I've got my beautiful orchid collection, porcelain eggs and the fish tank to care for. What more can a housewife wish for?" she said almost woefully.

She loved the idea of doing her hair up, putting on her favourite dress and make-up. Perhaps even pushing the boat out and wearing some of the sexy lingerie he'd kindly bought her over the years. Suddenly, she had to snap out of her parallel universe as she heard the frantic voice of her partner in crime.

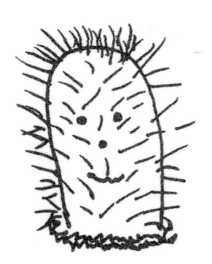

Gethin ran into the kitchen, shouting loudly and maniacally in a state of panic.

"Darling," she said calmly, "you really need to get a grip of yourself. After all, there's much more to life than weeding. Why don't you take up another hobby instead?" she suggested, trying to console her frustrated husband. "What about learning to Salsa dance?" She moved her hips tantalizingly, provocatively hoping he'd be enthusiastic about sharing a mutual hobby and an intimate one at that.

"You can't be serious, woman. I've spent years honing my skills for weeding and I'm most certainly not going to throw in the towel now. I need to pass on this irreplaceable talent and educate the next generation of budding *weeders* out there," he exclaimed. "Can't you see I have been blessed with this unique talent. I don't believe anyone else up here in the North can compare with my dedication and loyalty to my profession. Please don't mention this conversation again," he insisted. With that he buried his head in his hands.

He was almost in tears at the thought of his beautiful garden and work of art being terrorised by those obstinate nasty weeds. After a sharp intake of breath, he stood quaking in his boots, contemplating all the time he'd spent nurturing his beloved garden.

"Right, that's it!" he said suddenly. "This situation is extremely serious and I must take action immediately before it's too late. There's no time to waste. We cannot and will not be taken over," he said to himself, talking out loud as usual.

Just like his identical twin brother, Prof GD, *Beer Baron of the South*. He too had a serious obsession. More sensibly, perhaps, his was *Real Ales* and his mind was awash with more profitable satisfactions. Next to an eye for the ladies of course. Only the pretty ones, naturally.

They, the ageing twins, shared that idiosyncrasy of talking to themselves incessantly, a most annoying habit their respective spouses had endured over many years. And learnt to live with. Despite living virtually poles apart the two knew exactly what the other was thinking. Distance didn't make any difference to their intimate and unique communication. Well, sort of.

Prof GW was on another mission and that was to sort out his garden ahead of his forthcoming garden party. Well, if you are going to do it, you must do it in style. Particularly, when you live amongst almost Royal Fraternity.

"Right, that's it. I am on the case. However, I have a big job on my hands. I'm going to resolve this situation, and will not be defeated. Oh, no. I won't let this happen! It would be like the frightening 1951 story *The Day of the Triffids*, by John Wyndham. The famous post-apocalyptic novel about an aggressive species of plant which tried to take over the planet by killing people." He spoke with genuine fear in his voice.

Prof Gethin's situation was far less extreme. However, he was fast becoming paranoid and troubled to the point of virtual insanity. His weed obsession was growing to become a serious issue. Thankfully, with the love and support of his wife, he was going to get through this delusional period in his life. A mid-life crisis you might ask? Possibly. Or was it simply a case of PTSD?

"I know they're watching me from below, and secretly planning their attack," he said with trepidation. "Right, my darling. I'm off to Greenalls garden centre to stock up on my stash of *Devitas*, my chemical agent and partner in crime. With such a powerful defence, no weed will have a chance. I know it's so unlike me to forget the essentials on our weekly shopping list," he added shaking his head in disbelief.

Sally Anne, still the attractive and middle-aged desirable women, looked at her husband sadly, fearing the reality of the situation. Is he really losing the plot this time? she asked herself, trying to maintain her composure and her own sanity at the same time.

Well, I won't be bringing back any love gifts for Mrs W today. She does adore her hanging baskets, but I'm afraid my weeding is far more of a priority and the secret to our loving marriage of over forty years. I do wonder sometimes though. Perhaps being apart for most of the day gives us quality time together in the evenings. Ooh, and lots of lovings in the bedroom department, he thinks to himself with a smirk on his frustrated face.

Well, that's if you call watching boxed DVD sets of *Gardener's World* and David Attenborough documentaries exciting, supposed a somewhat frustrated Sally Anne.

Sally was more than happy to relax and watch a DVD of something humorous, *Mr Bean's Holiday* in particular. Watching ordinary TV channels was starting to depress lady Sally Anne.

"Oh, darling, I can't watch another programme about murder, murder and more bloody murders," she said with passion. "Why can't we go back to the good old days and watch something light like, *Ironside*, *Columbo* and all the rest of the day time schedule. My late grandmother adored all those programmes in her autumnal years. It's interesting, thinking back to when she was terminally ill. As time went on, she became so open, candid, honest and totally uninhibited within her thoughts. She used to tell me how she admired Ule Brinner. You know, the bald detective with the lollypop and deep voice. "What a talented actor he is," she would say to me with a grin on her face.

"Actually, I think she secretly fancied the actor. What was his name? Well, he would have resolved many of his cases if he had the deadly spray on board. Seriously. Think about it. Weapon in hand, no villain could escape. What an image. I can't think of anything more relaxing than putting my feet up with a glass or two of red wine and indulging in the colourful and wondrous lives of my favourite TV presenters. I feel they've become part of our family. There's obviously a synergy with our passion for the outdoors, he mused. I'd ideally love to meet them someday. Any of them. Who knows what the future will bring?" he asked himself with a glimmer of hope in his eyes. Well, he had previously met several famous personalities. But that wasn't enough.

As a small child his grandmother had taken him to meet the late Percy Thrower at his incredible garden centre on the outskirts of Birmingham.

"I remember the occasion well. Mr Thrower himself spent the entire day with me talking through his passion for plants and his love of all things green. The experience had a profound effect on my life as you can imagine. I didn't realise at the time, but my nan was a very good friend to Percy, but that's another story," he said out loud.

Prof GW clambered into his flat-based E-type Jaguar after waving goodbye to his much annoying and unwelcome garden pests, with a dire warning: "I'll be back with a vengeance. Don't you worry. You won't be going anywhere for now, but I'll have you later. Every single one of you. Can't wait to be weed free again." He rubbed his hands together with fiendish glee.

It was just a short drive to the vey exclusive and expensive garden centre on the edge of town.

Just to recap how the good professor had become acquainted with his local garden centre and his association with what would become his beloved *Devitas*. The first time he visited he hadn't known where to start. Not a clue. A cheerful young assistant wearing an identity badge proclaiming 'Paul', just plain and simple 'Paul' without a surname, had greeted him and asked what his requirements were.

"Of course, sir. Please follow me."

Then he guided him to the relevant aisle stacked with both weedkilling agents and fertilisers.

"There, sir. You'll surely find exactly what you're looking for."

Then Paul went on to explain that weeds are different to long, narrow blades of grass. They tend to be broad-leaved. So there were several varieties of weedkillers to suit a specific purpose.

"Yes. Yes. Yes. I fully understand that," he said, almost petulantly.

Then he looked at the stock before him and became somewhat perplexed. So much choice. Too much! Then one particular brand caught his eye. *Devitas*. Even here there were three types to choose from. The plastic containers were coloured and labelled. Red, blue and green, with bright orange tops and squirt guns After careful examination of each type he found the one which fitted the bill perfectly. *Devitas 'kills weeds not lawns'*, especially formulated for the eradication of weeds in grass lawns.

One which would kill clover, daisy, dandelion, and much more besides. Perfect. As you might say. Just what the doctor ordered. He was literally green with envy. And went away quite happily.

FAST FORWARD TO THE PRESENT

He soon arrived at the garden centre once again and parked his swanky Jaguar close to the entrance. He hurriedly ran towards his favourite aisle where he was welcomed by a familiar face.

A member of staff eager for his regular custom no doubt, a somewhat overzealous young assistant grinning like a Cheshire cat. The prof recognised Paul, who was all too familiar with his horticultural obsession with weeds over a number of years.

"Good morning, Professor. How are you today? Are those pesky *WEEDS* behaving themselves for you?"

Oh no! The young man hadn't quite realised what he'd innocently said. He'd put his big foot into the somewhat impossible situation.

"Well, quite honestly, not very happy at all Paul. I'm on the verge of a nervous breakdown. You're not going to believe it but my entire world feels as if it's falling down around me," he said dramatically. "I'm almost out of weedkiller. It's a real nightmare. Please can you help a nervous man in his hour of need?" he asked, almost pleading, with desperation in his voice.

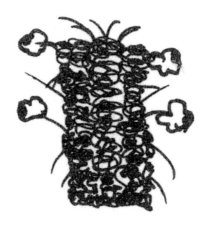

"Oh, dear me. I'm sorry to hear that, sir," he said, genuinely concerned for one of his favourite, most valued and loyal customers. "Please don't worry yourself, Professor. There must be something we can do to help," the assistant said, trying to reassure Mr W. "Right, let me think for a moment please. I'm confident we'll find a solution to this problem," he said enthusiastically.

"Okay, Professor. Please come with me," trying to calm Gethin down by making small talk about how busy the centre was at the moment.

"Well, it's the weather isn't it? As soon as the sun comes out everyone gets their green fingers ready for action. We're inundated with customers who are more than happy to spend their hard-earned cash here. What can I say?"

"The boss has a permanent smile on his face and doesn't have a bad word to say to any of us about delivering good quality customer service. We just can't do anything wrong and it's a pleasure to come to work," he said with pride written all over his youthful face.

They walked swiftly to the well-stocked aisle that housed the poisonous substance *Devitas*, amongst others. But, shock horror once again!

"Oh, no! Sir, we're clean out of stock and I'm afraid we won't be getting another delivery until the day after tomorrow at the earliest," he announced quite candidly.

"So what do you suggest I do? I won't be able to sleep tonight unless I have slaughtered those irritating growths that are making my life a misery," he bellowed outraged, and by now was an extremely angry Prof GW.

"Please may I make a suggestion? What about spraying on a strong solution of vinegar with warm water?" The young man was trying his best to resolve the problem to this deeply distressed man.

"What? Are you completely insane? Do you know anything about horticulture?" he barked with anger becoming redder and redder in the face as he addressed the now slightly bemused and fearful assistant.

Determined not to give up on this cantankerous elderly gentleman he calmly suggested, "OK, sir. Let's have a look to see if there are any suitable alternatives. Please come with me and we'll investigate."

By now Paul's patience was starting to wear thin, very thin, but he tried to remain cool, calm and collected, showing a great deal of professionalism.

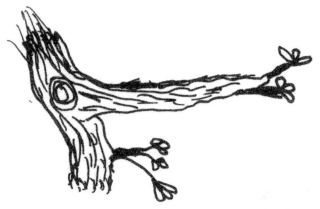

His boss, Manager Mark, would have been extremely proud of him, if only he had been a fly on the wall, so to speak. Deep down, Paul wanted to throttle this very, very demanding customer.

Ooh, he is such an annoying, antagonising pain in the backside, young Paul thought. Not to worry, he told himself. With that they walked down the aisles and thankfully found a crate or two of similar products, suitable as an emergency supply. Relief at last for such a difficult customer. But not exactly as Paul thought.

Forotegen.

"What on the earth is that?" asked the exasperated Professor. "I've never heard of it. Some cheap and nasty import no doubt," he said scathingly. By now, Weed Man was fast approaching his wit's end. "No! No! No!" he yelled in earshot of other bemused customers. "I was so looking forward to my daily routine. Instead, this has been a complete disaster. Goodness knows how high my bloody blood pressure is," said the irate prof.

Calm down, calm down, Paul told himself.

By now Prof GW was starting to draw attention to himself as other customers were intrigued by all the commotion. Well, after all, this was a highly respected establishment full of very wealthy and well–to-do locals. This outrageous scene was unexpected, so out of the ordinary.

"Calm down please, Professor. Please. Please. I'm only trying to help. And would you be kind enough to stop raising your voice. People are watching."

"I'm sincerely sorry, Paul. I didn't mean to be so rude. I appreciate your time and trouble along with your patience," he said wagging his tail between his legs. "It's just that carrying the prestigious title of *King of the Weed Killers* in our local community means so much to me. I'm such a very proud man. The honorary role gives me privy to so many high-profile functions and I'm regarded as somewhat of a celebrity. You must understand that my reputation could be on the line if I don't keep up appearances and maintain the high standards of my immaculate garden. You know I've held the title for ten years in succession and I intend holding on to my golden *Weed* trophy and accolade for the duration," he added with pride and passion in his voice. "You're such a young man with your entire future ahead of you. All I have now I'm retired is being at one with nature after a long and stressful career in a high profile and powerful position within the Secret Service." He slumped, visibly shaken, with a sad tone in his voice. "If only I could share some of my memoirs with you. Unfortunately, I've been sworn to secrecy. It's frustrating at times because I'd love to be able to spill the beans with my wonderful wife, Sally Anne. But I just can't. I know you might think I'm slightly paranoid and possibly bonkers. However, there's much you don't know or understand how the agency operates. In some ways I miss being a government agent. I had to be very disciplined and regimented in so many ways. Not always a pleasant experience. I can tell you. Now, I'm no longer required, superfluous to requirements, I feel as though I'm on the scrap heap of life. I needed to throw myself into a hobby and treat it like one of my major tasks." He continued pouring his heart out to this slightly bemused young man.

Then the professor quickly changed the subject and returned to reality and the present day. "People come from far and wide to enjoy the fruits of my labour. The *Weed* free garden is my pride and joy and it's a pleasure to share with others who appreciate it," he added.

"I'm sorry, but I didn't understand how important your *Weeding* meant to you, sir. Well, it's not exactly up there in the top ten of hobbies is it?" Paul asked feeling a little uncomfortable by this passionate declaration of love for this man's *Weeding*.

"Oh, yes. The local school children have been here having researched the garden for their after-school projects; also, senior citizens from the hospice down the road. I've even had the top gardening experts and TV and radio presenters film a one-off special about me, entitled: *How To Love Your Garden*. Yes. I was interviewed throughout the programme by the best of the bunch. Mr Alan Titchmarsh and Ms Charlie Dimmock. It was a wonderful experience being in the limelight for a day. Hard work though," he stressed. "Oh, I almost forgot. I even had a visit from the celebrity TV gardener and award winner from South Wales. He weekly runs his shows from his allotment. That talented gent knows his subject too. What a nice bloke. Shame I can't recall his name," he added, feeling a little embarrassed.

"Oh, that sounds very interesting. So you *are* a real TV star, a celebrity then?" Paul asked excitedly?

"Well, not exactly, but I did receive a small fee, some beautiful pot plants and most importantly, a good supply of *WEEDKILLER*. What else can a green-veined man want?"

He questioned the young man, who rather sheepishly said, "Please can I just ask you, sir, who is Ms CD?" He was intrigued.

"Oh, she's the one with the enormous knockers who doesn't wear a bra on screen. That surely contributes to the massive viewing figures," he said, in quite a matter-of-fact manner winking at the assistant.

"Wow. I'll have to look her up when I get home. There's bound to be something about her on *Facebook*," he replied, with an excited and somewhat smug grin on his face.

Trying to stop fantasising about Charlie Dimmock, Paul came back to reality, slightly flushed in the face.

"Professor Weed. I've just had a light-bulb moment. Why don't you go on-line and order your *Devitas* that way? The company will deliver within twenty-four hours or you can, I believe, fast track for a small fee," he suggested with a glimmer of hope.

By now the harassed assistant was beginning to lose the will to live. Well, so to speak. "Just an idea, sir," he added shrugging his shoulders in utter despair.

"*Yes, yes, yes*, you clever young man. Why didn't I think of that? I'll go straight home and start surfing the net. Oh, I haven't done this before. Is it difficult for a man of my maturing years?" he asked the helpful Paul.

"I don't think you will have any problems, sir," he replied. Oh dear.

"Thank you so much, for your help. Here, put this ten pounds in your pocket and treat yourself and one of your friends to a well-deserved drink on me. After all, you've had to listen to me prattle on and on about my weed killer dilemma," he said kindly.

"Thanks, Professor. Good luck on your mission. Please come back and let me know how you get on. I look forward to seeing you soon. Perhaps you might invite me to visit your famous weed free garden in the future."

"Well, I'm hoping that with a little help from my friends we might be able to pull off a little garden party in the summer. What do you think? Well, it won't be quite like the VIP do our monarch hosts, but it will be something special. With your assistance of course," he remarked with a huge grin on his face.

Off went the very jubilant *SERIAL WEED KILLER* with hope in his heart. For the time being.

He couldn't wait to get on to the Internet and make his first ever purchase online, but first he had to complete a very important task…

A ritual very close to Prof Weed's heart.

The Weed Walk of the year. Really. Sounds strange, but it occurred annually in the locality on the official first day of spring. This was also part of his ritual involving a meticulous investigation of the garden in order to identify any rogue greens. With his industrial-sized magnifying glass, he was a man on yet another mission. To him a vital mission, no less.

All was well and harmonious at the Weed Ranch and both Prof and Mrs W enjoyed a relaxing evening together watching DVD's about *How to care for your lawns*. Exciting viewing. Hmm. And off to bed.

The house was filled with peace, harmony and tranquillity until… Around eight a.m. there was a sharp, rasping knock on the door.

"Who the hell can that be at this time of the morning? We aren't expecting the postman with anything are we dear?" he asked curiously. Mrs Weedall was still in the land of nod. No response there. Lucky woman. Prof Weedall went downstairs to investigate.

He was late for his usual investigation this morning. He'd forgotten to set the alarm clock. Most out of character for the pedantic good professor.

Prof GW was perplexed asking himself, What has Mrs W been up to this time? And more importantly, why do we need a three-ton truck outside? Oh dear, I remember the last time she impetuously bought items online. It was that dreadful wooden summer house that took me the best part of eight weeks to put together. Then it rained incessantly for days and the roof leaked terribly. She blamed me for not using the waterproof felt. I had looked at it, but used it as a floor mat instead. Obviously wrong! It was a situation bordering on divorce, he conceded.

Oh, and there was her obsession with the hats she'd bought over the years. Not satisfied with one or two smart hats like most women, her huge hat collection piled high on top of the bedroom wardrobe. Nearly thirty at the last count, I believe. And all the expensive patent leather shoes and boots she'd regularly purchased from A.G. Meeks of Cardiff. Surely, she hasn't developed OCD like myself with my nuisance weeds I hope, he thought wistfully.

He came back to reality with a bump when the delivery driver persistently rang the doorbell and hammered on the door.

He started to shake, worried about what to expect. He gave out an enormous yawn then answered the door.

"Good morning to young man," he said jovially.

"Yep, I guess so," the delivery man said in a matter-of-fact way. "Look, mate. We need to get this gear off the truck ASAP. Another job to do round the corner in ten. Where do you want this lot dumped?" he asked.

Prof GW thought hurriedly and suggested whatever the unexpected contents of the container were, he would welcome the delivery drivers to deposit it in the garden and garage.

That decision turned out to be a poor one. A very poor one.

In hindsight and if he had been thinking straight, he should have insisted that he hadn't placed an order with them and asked them to return the delivery to the depot.

It wasn't as straightforward as that though.

The two hefty guys, tattoos up to their armpits, came dragging along dozens of wooden crates stacked with no end of sacks.

This was all becoming a complete mystery to Prof GW. "What on earth is in those enormous containers?" he repeatedly asked himself.

He went up to the delivery chaps and asked them what had been delivered in such an enormous lorry, 'Greenalls Garden Centre' clearly embossed on both sides of the enormous truck.

'Well, mate, this is your order from eBay. Crikey, you must have one hell of a lot of *weeds* to kill. This lot will keep you going for years and years to come," he said laughing, while shaking his head knowingly.

Prof GW was starting to feel nervous, very nervous. He was not the sort of person to panic easily and was renowned for keeping a cool head. His training in the Secret Service taught him to be always calm and collective. But this was just too much for him to take. He threw his hands in the air in disbelief, with a sense of hopelessness.

He hesitatingly opened one of the twenty-four crates to discover 2448 bags of the weedkiller. Yes. 2448 bags of the wretched stuff — *Devitas*.

"Goodness gracious me. Only a madman could have purchased such a huge amount of the stuff. No one in their right mind would have done something so foolish," he exclaimed loudly.

Obviously, he was oblivious to the foolish error of his ways the previous day. For the time being at least. Clearly, he was living on the edge of sanity.

Heaven hopes there might be a solution to this dreadful scenario. He prayed silently to some mysterious god who had obviously forsaken him in his hour of need.

Prof GW woefully signed the delivery note and again started to tremble with fear, almost at his wits' end.

"Oh, dear me. What have I done?" He was very frightened as to how Mrs W was going to react to this farcical scenario. Well, in actual fact it was a very serious situation and Prof GW needed to think on his feet quickly in order to put things right, if at all possible.

How am I going to explain? I must have had one too many glasses of wine before ordering online. Well, I hadn't done it before and it seemed so easy. The wife's going to make my life hell on earth and probably seek a divorce. I can feel it. Either that or she's going to hit me over the head with a blunt instrument and watch me die slowly in terrible pain. He felt one of his panic attacks coming on yet again.

Meanwhile, Mrs W was up and about and curious as to where her two hard-boiled eggs were. Not one on the table in its usual china egg-cup at the usual breakfast time. "This has been our morning ritual for over forty years," she told herself. "This is just not on. Where *is* my breakfast? More importantly what is that psychotic husband of mine doing?" she wondered.

Mrs Weedall, Sally Anne, was a caring, loving wife and mother. However, she did like to be treated like a princess at the breakfast table. That meant a lot to her. Ever since they married, Gethin had always prepared a sumptuous spread for his adorable wife. He'd never failed to deliver on time. Every morning. So what was the reasoning behind his lapse in preparing for the first meal of the day? Sally Anne become curious. Worse still, very suspicious.

Well after forty-plus years with someone you get to know their little habits of a lifetime, one of which was her husband's regular visits to the comfort station. Yes. I know. The bathroom to you and me. Sometimes he would spend almost a whole hour in there, reading the daily papers. What else?

Sally Anne busied herself in the kitchen whilst planning her day ahead. She was going to meet up with her best friend, Gloria, for a coffee and a catch-up of the latest women's gossip. This was a regular rendezvous where both ladies got the opportunity to tell all regarding their respective husbands' foibles. Oh, if only those two, *femme fatale* could have put down on paper the things they discussed. X-rated or what?

Back to Prof GW. He was not having a good start to the day. Poor old chap.

"This isn't turning out to be the perfect day I'd predicted. I woke up this morning with the sun shining, birds tweeting in the trees and now I feel my life is about to end in tragedy, just like an episode of *Midsummer Murders*," he muttered.

He was starting to fall apart mentally and feeling like a caged animal, a rabbit in the glare of dazzling oncoming headlights.

"Oh dear. What am I going to do?" he asked himself repeatedly in deep desperation.

As he predicted and on cue, out came Mrs W, only to discover their beautiful lawns and patio had been transformed into an enormous garden centre.

Oh dear!

Discovering the gargantuan supply of chemical was just going one *weed* too far. She thought hard and longingly.

"Your obsession has taken its toll on me and I'm not standing for it. Enough is enough," she said shaking like a leaf. "I've had it up to here with your insane behaviour," she declared. "Go and get the tent from the attic and then you can be close to your beloved weeds all night and day long. Have fun," she added tearfully. And stormed back indoors, slamming the back door behind her.

Well after all there was no room for him in the garage due to the colossal bags of *Devitas*.

After a restless night's sleep in the tent, Prof GW woke up with his head spinning.

"I'm determined to rectify this situation. More importantly I need to save my marriage. There's no problem that can't be solved," he declared with some optimism.

Having a quick shower back in the house he cleared his mind and planned the day ahead. He felt relaxed, invigorated and full of vitality.

Another day, another dollar, he calmly thought. Little did he know what the day ahead was to present.

"Well, today can't be any worse than yesterday, can it?" he asked himself, feeling extremely confident in his ability to turn a negative situation into a positive one.

He boiled two free-range eggs for his beloved Mrs W. Decorated the table with a few of the finest red roses which he displayed in a delicate and expensive Waterford crystal glass vase purchased from a rather posh shop in York the previous year. Not forgetting the bread-and-butter, orange juice, salt and pepper. Oh, and her six prunes. They always got her going in the morning.

Yes. That looks the part he thought. Looking quite proud of his small but significant gesture.

"Blimey, I need to earn some brownie points today. I want so much to be back in the loving arms of my wife. I miss her so much," he said sadly.

With treats in mind, he put his thinking cap on. Okay I feel another visit to the garden centre coming on. I just hope I can retain my composure and avoid any embarrassing behaviour after my previous display of emotion. I can't afford to make a spectacle of myself again.

His mind rewound to the previous day when he'd had an outburst with an unpredictable audience, most of whom were probably from his neighbourhood. He felt deflated and ashamed but determined to hold his head up high.

Prof GW couldn't face talking to his weeds this morning. Oh no. He was far too preoccupied with the huge problem he had to overcome, regarding his humongous stock of *Devitas*.

Whilst unable to sleep in the tent within the grounds of his family home, Prof GW had an idea. Well, a cunning plan you could say.

He'd decided to try and camouflage the entire stock of *weedkiller* with some sort of canopy, tarpaulin or waterproof fabric. Just to keep prying eyes away from the monstrous mountain.

It's off to the garden centre again. This is becoming my second home, he thought. Well, he wasn't far wrong. For this would prove the beginning of a long-term if unexpected relationship.

Off he went and after just a couple of miles he was there. Yet again.

He parked his car some distance away from the main entrance hoping no one would recognise it. Donning a pair of designer sunglasses and a rather smart flat cap, he hoped no one would see him

He assumed his disguise would allow easy access to the particular aisle he was heading for. He certainly didn't need or want to be stopped by some of the neighbours he only knew too well, who could talk for England. As a proud Welshman with humble roots, he thought them best avoided. Just in case.

I hope I don't bump into that polite and pleasant young man again. What on earth would he think of me? Just a foolish, pathetic old man who'd only gone and purchased and probably depleted all stock of *Devitas* on eBay. Mmm. He pondered.

He walked briskly towards the area that stocked all the waterproof materials when suddenly he heard a very familiar voice. Yes. It was the jovial young assistant Paul.

Oh no! Another nightmare. However, this chance encounter with Paul would eventually turn out to be a very positive one. It was meant to be. And his saving grace.

"Good morning, Professor. Pleased to see you again so soon. Thank you for your kind tip. Suzie, my girlfriend and I enjoyed a drink or two outside the Green Bell pub. The sun was shining and it was a relaxing way to end our working day." The Prof didn't respond to that comment as his mind was elsewhere.

"Right. Please give me the latest update on your *Devitas* situation. How did you get on with eBay? I understand it can be a little frustrating when ordering online for the first time, but I'm sure you're able to circumnavigate your way around," he said confidently.

Once again young Paul had said the wrong thing. Unbeknown to him Prof GW had unfortunately made a dastardly mistake.

The prof's tongue dried up and he felt an enormous lump in his throat.

What can I say to this young man who's gone out of his way to assist me with on mission impossible? I'm going to be a laughing stock and thought of as the village idiot. Well, that's how I'm beginning to feel, he told himself again shaking his head in disbelief.

He stood in front of young Paul, considering this awkward moment in time. Speechless for just a while, he looked into his eyes and, having taken a sharp intake of breath he exhaled slowly. Before he knew it, he had inadvertently blurted out everything. He had to confide in someone and obviously it wasn't going to be his wife, Sally Anne. But to a stranger? Yes.

Paul couldn't stop quietly laughing. He was verging on the point of hysteria.

Prof GW gave a sigh of relief as Paul tried to regain his composure, having the odd giggle intermittently at the good man's expense. Understandable, really.

"Look, my friend, I've got more than just my reputation to think about. This situation is far more serious. My wife is threatening to divorce me if I don't resolve the situation," he said with dismay. Licking his wounds and begging for help at the same time.

"Leave it with me, Professor. I have an idea. Can't promise to wave a magic wand but there are a few thoughts running through my mind as we speak. Please take a seat in the patio area and help yourself to a cup of coffee courtesy of the management," he said, trying once again to console the nervous man.

Paul wasted no time. He too had a serious problem which needed fixing ASAP. He was having difficulty resolving his problem of undelivered goods for several other clients. So off he went to seek the expert advice of Mark Bushall, his manager. He knocked the door of his office and was welcomed in. The ongoing plight of Professor GW was then discussed in great detail. No stone unturned.

They both had such a laugh, almost falling off their seats thinking about the situation.

"What a carry on," they both joked. However, there was some twisted logic behind what they'd just inadvertently said: *Carry on Weeding* would make a brilliant title for a follow-up from the many hilarious films produced by Peter Rogers," suggested manager Mark. They both started to giggle again. Surprise. Surprise.

Of course, it wasn't at the good prof's expense. No. Not totally. They both were determined to sort out this major problem. Mark had spent his entire career in the retail trade and had never encountered such a ludicrous situation. He had no answer. What to do? Then, in a light-bulb moment, he knew.

Perhaps, just possibly, he may have also found a solution to their own unexpected in-house problem.

"These things happen. It's far too easy to do what he did. You need to know and understand the Internet. If you don't, it can quite easily take over your life in so many ways. Poor Prof W. I really feel for Mrs W. I wonder how she's coping with this crazy situation. Right, Paul. I've got a proposition for our very good friend," said the caring manager, Mark. "Just give me a few moments please to write up some notes and I'll be with you shortly," he said. "Where can I find you both?"

"We're outside, sitting in the patio area. I've given him a complimentary coffee. Hope that's okay, Boss," he enquired.

"Not a problem. You're doing a grand job, young man. Thanks for going over and above your duties. This'll be noted in your appraisal portfolio, I promise. Well done," he added, smiling from ear-to-ear.

The good prof felt relaxed, unusually relaxed, enjoying the peaceful ambience of familiar surroundings. He was, in essence, very much like a child in a sweet shop. An extremely large sweet shop to him. He was surrounded by all things *garden*. He was in his element. From patio furniture, decorative decking and fancy lighting to beautiful pot plants and miniature trees and shrubbery.

Ooh. This is the life, he thought somewhat contentedly.

His mind drifted to home and his ongoing project to create the ultimate haven within his own beautiful garden. A pure sanctuary, a place of escapism away from the pressures of daily life.

Suddenly, he was brought back to reality with the sound of familiar voices. It was his new-found friend, Paul the salesman, along with Mark the garden centre manager.

"Hello, Professor W. Good to see you again. Paul's been telling me all about your little problem and tale of woe. Fear not. This is completely between the three of us and I can reassure you it will go no further," he said reassuringly. "After all, if the press got a whiff of this potential story it could destroy us all," he said in a matter-of-fact tone of voice. "Paul and I have been in discussion about how we might be able to offer a solution to your current crisis. Please hear me out. Between the two of us we think we might have come up with a potential action plan to this situation. Firstly, we too have a very serious problem on our hands. Our delivery of *Devitas* has been cancelled by our suppliers. No reason, just an email to say we're off their list. Well, we have no contingency plan in place. This leaves us in a very difficult position. And we don't quite know how to cope with it. As you may be aware, we're part of a UK wide chain and we depend on reliable sources to keep us well stocked on all our products. It's so frustrating. Secondly, our customers, like your good self, are frustrated and looking to our competitors for one of our most popular products. Obviously, we can't afford to lose their business. *Weedkiller* is one of our most sought-after products along with fertilisers, with keen gardeners like yourself," he explained feeling frustrated.

He then changed his tone of voice and without any sense of malice continued. "I hope you know where this conversation is going Professor," he said confidently.

"Well, excuse me, Mark, but I really don't understand your serious dilemma. But how can I help? Please explain," said a slightly confused professor.

Quite ironic that such a highly intelligent and educated man couldn't see the potential business proposition that was lying on the table in front of him.

"Well, it's quite simple really. We're offering to purchase your excessive stock of *Devitas* at the current retail price. Collect and deposit within our stores with no charge," he added. "This leaves you with a significant profit on your original eBay purchase. In addition, you will get your garden space back. Much to the delight of Mrs W no doubt," he added with a smile of hope on his face. "Obviously, you'll be helping us tremendously by having a ready supply of *Devitas* to hand, plus the fact we won't have to consider distribution fees from our original, over-greedy suppliers. "So what do you say? Is it a deal, or no deal?" asked manager Mark in anticipation of the correct answer.

"Let me have a little think, please," said the Prof GW, unintentionally keeping Mark in suspense.

Curiously, he was shaking with excitement. Nothing he'd known for years. Pound signs and more pound signs flashed before his eyes in disbelief. He was in a win-win situation, and being offered an opportunity he couldn't possibly refuse. He'd have been a fool not to  bite his hand off. He put his thinking cap on and soberly contemplated this once in a lifetime opportunity. Well, I can't afford to make any more foolish decisions," he contemplated. "Can you just make it categorically clear please. Are you telling me that by agreeing to this deal I'll be making over a forty-five percent profit on my original purchase?" asked a curious professor.

"Yes. No hidden agenda. Just a straightforward business transaction," Mark said trying to reassure the somewhat nervous professor.

"Of course. This makes perfect sense. You have presented me with an opportunity I cannot refuse. Our arrangement could possibly save my marriage. I can't thank you enough," he said gratefully. "When this is all over, I intend hosting a little garden party to celebrate our success at the weed free garden of the North. I do sincerely hope both Paul, his girlfriend, and of course yourself and good lady, will come along," he insisted.

The two shook hands and it was all stations go.

"Down to business it is then. I just need your bank details etc and then we are up and running. We'll transfer the funds just after we receive delivery. Could we collect this afternoon if this is convenient, Professor? I'll send one of our trucks to you around two p.m. Is this all right with you?" he enquired.

"Not a problem at all. Thank you so very much for the opportunity to work with you and for saving my skin," said the jubilant prof, now an extremely satisfied customer. With the meeting complete Mark returned to his office to get the ball rolling.

"Young Paul, you have been my hero in my darkest of hours and I will always be grateful for your help. Here take this." Prof GW handed Paul

two fifty pound notes and shoved them in his hand. "It's not a huge amount considering the profit I have made on this deal. I did make the most ludicrous purchase and a very stupid decision," he said with a slightly high-pitched voice. "However, *you* have saved the day."

"No, sir I cannot accept your kind generosity. It's company policy you see," he insisted. "I could be dismissed if anyone found out."

"Stuff that nonsense. Just let me slip it into your pocket when no one is watching. Go on, take that nice girl of yours out to the pictures. Oh, and make hay while the sun is shining," he insisted.

Paul started to blush, his cheeks as red as beetroot. "Thank you, Professor. I'm so glad we were able to *Devitas* the problem," he said chuckling, "I hope you and Mrs W make up, and have a wonderful evening."

"Well, that's the plan, Paul. I think I have a fair bit of grovelling to do though. I'll keep you updated," he said with a nervous grin on his face. "Oh, and Paul, please from now on call me Gethin," he added.

An ecstatic professor walked back to the car feeling almost punch drunk.

"I don't believe it. What a difference a day makes, indeed," he said to himself, feeling that familiar song coming on.

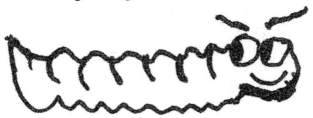

"This calls for a celebration. Off to the supermarket to stock up on some special fine food and wines. Perhaps some chocolate liqueurs, French bread and a selection of fine cheeses. Wensleydale medium crumbly white, soft Gouda, White Stilton and blue-veined Cheshire blue, amongst others. Not forgetting that Mrs W is especially fond of that Greek Feta cheese," he said with uncontrollable excitement. "I must get all those for her and Jacobs Cream Crackers. Oh, and that Italian red wine she enjoys. Monteputio De

Bruzo. I can't let her have too much on an empty tummy though it makes her nasty. Mind you, on the other hand if I ply her with a sumptuous buffet, she'll just get amorous. That sounds more like it. Oh, I can't wait," he said excitedly, acting like someone who had just discovered he'd won the National Lottery. "I'm starting to get excited now. Just hope I can get it right. I'm only going to get one chance at this so I had better pull out all the stops." He had butterflies in his stomach and shaking with nerves as well.

The prof was becoming anxious as he drove towards his home. He disliked deceiving his beloved because they were and always had been open and honest with each other throughout their marriage, Now Gethin was under pressure to get his master plan underway.

Well, he was entering unknown territory. He had no control over the unpredictable course of events that were ahead of him.

What do I do or say to Sally Anne? And, where do I start to tell her about my ordeal? His hands trembled and legs felt like jelly, at the thought of facing her.

Well for goodness sake, I'm not a criminal, far from it. I just want to make up with Sally Anne and put things right.

He was beating himself up about his foolish actions, but hopefully he was doing the right thing. He was prepared to do anything to win back the love of his life.

What about popping across to York and buying her a sexy nightie or something? he wondered.

Back to reality. He had to park up just outside the main entrance to his drive to allow the expected three-ton lorry access.

He walked into the kitchen to face the music. Well. He was on a high and so pleased with himself about his successful meeting and accomplishments.

I can't wait to tell Mrs W. She won't believe our luck.

Then he paused for thought moment.

No, I'm not going to tell her. Not yet anyway. I'll get her out of the house this afternoon so she doesn't have to experience all the commotion.

Once the job is done, I'll surprise her with a VIP picnic on the patio.

As he thought about his next plan of action his mobile rang. Ironically, it was Mrs W.

"Hi," she said calmly. "Just to let you know I'm meeting Gloria in York instead of town. I may be a little later than planned. Probably three to three thirty. Is that Okay?" she asked in her familiar gentle tone.

Trying to contain his emotions and disguise his slightly squeaky high-pitched voice at the same time, he replied, "Oh, thank you for letting me know," he added with sheer elation. "That's not a problem. Please send my love to Grumpy Gloria," he added with a smirk.

"See you later then. I'm looking forward to it," added Sally Anne.

Sally Anne and Gloria Honeydew were the best of friends at the local comprehensive school many years ago. Sally Anne went on to university to study chemistry, which was where she met a handsome young fellow student, Gethin David Weedall. They quickly fell in love and a few years later happily married, and remained a contented, loving couple. Gethin became a lecturer and higher things beckoned. He became targeted by the Secret Service for his special skills in martial arts. Gloria went to training college and became a primary school teacher.

Inevitably, the two women drifted apart to pursue vastly different pathways through life. They were of completely different temperaments. Gloria was a larger-than-life character, full of energy, exuberance and very much outgoing, and a flirt. Very much so. Sally Anne, on the other hand was softly spoken and modest, almost shy.

Only a few years ago the former girls happened to bump into each other while shopping in York, where they rekindled their former friendship. They agreed to meet up once a month, there to relive past memories and chat about their lives and marriages over a coffee or, more frequently, a glass or two of red wine. Yes. Female gossip at its most prolific. What's new?

Prof GW couldn't stand brazen Gloria, with her wildly kept long hair and red pouting lips. She was too full of herself and he considered her nothing more than a tart and busybody, a know-all. And he found it difficult to be polite. Not surprisingly, perhaps, Gloria considered him pompous, dismissive and just plain rude. But he never objected to the two of them keeping contact. As long as he was kept out of the equation. Totally.

Now Prof GW knew Sally Anne was up to something with that awful friend of hers, but he didn't care. Not a damn. He had a mountain to climb before she arrived home.

Oh, and a very big thank you to whoever is looking down on me. I'm really going to make this work, he told himself over and over again. Was it a vain hope? Mmm.

The phone lay silent and Gethin began to calm down from what had been a fast, furious, and quite eventful morning.

Then there was a knock on the door. He looked out to see that Greenalls Garden Centre lorry had arrived. Its logo emblazoned on both sides. A little bit earlier than expected, but so far so good. His plan was going smoothly. The chaps were there to collect the excess weedkiller. 'Halleluiah!' He rejoiced.

Professor Weedall answered the door to greet two very well-built chaps. There it was, the three-ton truck parked in the driveway. Difficult to hide one of those from the nosy neighbours.

Does it matter though and who cares what they think? he considered.

"Hi there, mate. Here to collect your stock," the taller of the pair said, half-laughing.

Obviously, the good prof was the talk of the garden centre, but GW didn't mind. After all, these events could only add to his popularity as *Serial Weed Killer of the North.*

It's all public relations at the end of the day. If this situation turns around as planned, perhaps I'll issue a press release to the quality national papers. Perhaps even sell my story for a princely sum. The prof was getting ahead of himself and becoming a little overconfident. Let's hope his action plan doesn't backfire.

He was well on the way to putting things right and he was feeling good.

"Good to see you so quickly. Please let yourselves in through the back gate. Do you need a hand with anything? A cup of coffee or a cold drink?" he asked enthusiastically.

"No thanks, mate. Cheers for asking though. Everything is sorted. Just sign the collection paperwork, Okay?"

Ten minutes later the hard-working guys were gone and there was no evidence of the superfluous order of *Devitas* anywhere. It seemed like a miracle. Prof GW jumped for joy, elated by the fact that his little bit of cunning may have just paid off. "Haha, teehee," he laughed out loud.

One job complete. All that remained was to do the food shop, one of the weekly chores he thoroughly enjoyed. Retail therapy he called it. Yes. Rightly so.

I feel like a naughty school boy. I just hope Mrs W enjoys the feast I am going to prepare for her in our special place.

I'm trying my best and enjoying every minute of it. Let's hope I can crack that hard shell of hers and that she'll once again expose her soft centre. That's given me some food for thought. I must put a box of chocolates on the list. And mint creams of course, he thought wistfully.

He was getting a little carried away by now as the adrenalin was pumping and his entire body was quivering with excitement.

Prof GW got in the car, and feeling slightly high on life, drove to the local supermarket. He couldn't stop thinking about how Mrs W was going to react to his romantic gesture.

I do hope she'll forgive me and welcome me back into her loving arms.

Arriving at the shops, he started thinking about what goodies he needed to purchase for his romantic feast. No, exotic feast. Well, he hadn't prepared a list. Like most men. He was in dangerous uncharted territory. Again.

Stop and think, Gethin, he told himself.

All logic went out the window as he began filling his trolley with all sorts of extravagant treats for the love banquet to be. Before long it was almost half full, leaving just enough room for the essentials. Toilets rolls. Wine, beer and of course Champagne.

Feeling satisfied with his purchases he had an afterthought.

I must stop off at the florist and buy a beautiful exotic orchid to add to Mrs W's collection. And a piece of sexy lingerie from the shop next door. "If that doesn't win her over, I can't think what will," he said out loud not realizing the customers in the queue were listening with bemusement. Wearing huge smiles on their faces. They all seemed moved by his expression of sentimentality.

"Hello there! We couldn't help wondering what the occasion is. You're obviously going to spoil your good lady and lucky her," enquired the little old dear wearing a hearing aid standing behind him.

"Oh, it's just something I do from time to time. My wife is always running around after me so it's payback time once a month," he explained, dodging the real issue. Well, he hadn't got all day to pour his heart out and share his life story in five minutes.

After paying up and packing there was just enough time for a quick detour to the local florist where he purchased the most exquisite of purple orchids they had in stock. He knew Sally Anne would love it. Oddly, she too had her slightly eccentric nature. She'd water her treasured orchids once a week. But was it normal to stand each plant in water using their kitchen egg-timer to measure six minutes to the second before draining off the excess liquid?

Finally, a visit to the sumptuous lingerie shop. He was greeted by a very glamorous female assistant who was more than obliging and eager to assist the eager professor. "May I ask what you are looking for, sir?"

Well, after what seemed like half an hour explaining his predicament, she smiled and blushed trying to remain professional, but secretly wanted to laugh out loud.

This poor man seriously needs my help, she thought.

She began thinking about the actor Rowan Atkinson's hilarious character, Mr Bean — who else — comparing him to this unfortunate customer who was obviously no stranger to self-inflicted disastrous situations.

This man is so like him, she thought to herself smiling.

The glamorous assistant helped Prof GW choose a very special bedtime surprise for Sally Anne.

"What's your wife's favourite colour, please?" she asked curiously.

"Red, red and more red!" he announced with much excitement. "After all, red is far more than for danger. It's equally true for romantic passion," he blurted out.

"Ah! Right. I've got the perfect gift for you, and your wife of course," she remarked with a very knowingly cheeky glint in her eyes.

It was a bright red, sheer see-through negligee. Prof GW was salivating at the thought of Mrs W wearing this saucy little number.

Then he noticed the price tag. "Oh no. It's a bit on the expensive side," he considered, wrinkling his nose in Mr Bean fashion. "But she's worth it. Thank you, young lady, you've been very helpful. I am sure Mrs Weedall, that's my wife, Sally Anne, will be more than delighted with my purchase," he announced, somewhat nervously. Not quite getting his words out in the correct order.

On his way out of the shop he happened to glance at a section devoted to menswear. And some very strange outfits. Sausage and two veg jock straps and mankini posing pouches. He'd never heard of them before, let alone seen them, though he'd hardly lived a sheltered life. He looked at the mankinis. What? A very small piece of stretched material 'to fit all sizes'. So it said on the packaging blurb.  And guess what? He spotted one in green. His favourite colour. Should he, or shouldn't he? Would this skimpy, all too brief garment arouse, excite even his rather staid wife? He dithered. Then *yes*. He would buy it. Which he did. After all, it was far more reasonably priced than the women's ensemble for sale.

On handing it back, lovingly wrapped, the young assistant gave him a strange look and burst out laughing. Prof GW went bright red in the face with embarrassment, and hurriedly left the shop.

Wasn't he a bit over the hill for that sort of thing? she wondered. Which made her day. I hope that gentleman has a bit more luck tonight. He deserves it after all he has been through today, she mused.

She had something comical to tell her mates in the pub that evening, who didn't believe a word of it. Fancy that. How about you?

With his delightful gifts beautifully wrapped he headed back to the love nest.

He was feeling proud as punch with his achievements.

It was early afternoon, two forty-five p.m. to be precise and thank goodness Mrs W was nowhere to be seen.

"Good, I've got the kitchen all to myself. I'd better get started. The day can only get better," he repeatedly told himself.

Prof GW put on his fish-themed apron and, of course, with the company of Barry White playing in the background. Well, he had to set the mood just right for this momentous occasion.

He started preparing for the sumptuous feast. A very indulgent picnic to say the least. You could say it was going to be fit for a queen. His queen. His beautiful Sally Anne. He was in his element now and firing on all four cylinders. Full throttle, and feeling well-pleased with himself.

The only ingredient missing from the mix of hors d'oeuvres, prawn cocktail, salad and cheeses was his good lady. Well, it was vital to keep her at bay so as not to spoil the special surprise.

Whilst preparing the culinary delights, he began reminiscing about how he'd proposed to Mrs W all those years ago. This afternoon was going to be equally romantic, if not a celebration to remember in future years to come.

"I just want to make it up to my beloved. Over the years I feel I've neglected her in favour of my passion for being *King of The Weed Killers in the North*."

All that remained was to decorate the patio table with the cloth he'd just purchased from the shops, embossed with bright red hearts, along with matching serviettes. A little tacky, but I know it will put a smile on her face, he thought.

The only problem was that the cloth was far too long for the table. That didn't really matter to him. But…

I know. I'll have to put my thinking cap on, he declared. I'll get the pinking shears from the garage and cut around to give that zigzag look. Yes! It's all coming together. If I get any more excited though I think I might just explode. There's something missing. Yes! I need to get the hostess trolley out here and put our *Lazy Susan* on it ready for the dips. Oh, and the ice bucket for the Champagne.

Prof GW placed the trolley *in situ* and covered it with yet another, smaller, disposable table cloth. The cooler filled with ice and all the sumptuous foods covered with cling film made quite an impressive display.

"Oh, my taste buds are tingling and I feel temptation to sample all these delicious delicatessen delights. No, I mustn't. Show some will power and restrain yourself," he told himself.

Gethin W had excelled himself and was feeling quite pleased, and rightly so.

"So here we go," he said aloud. "Kitchen clean and tidy. Champagne on ice, check. Quiches. Pâté. Oh I've forgotten the cheesecake. Hopefully she won't notice. All on board with chilled white wine on the table. With the best crystal glasses."

Then he thought, oh, that's not a good idea. There might be a small problem as Sally Anne never uses the best cut glasses. Of course they are for display purposes only. Okay. Let's get those back in the cabinet and replace them with the cheaper everyday ones. She won't notice the difference after a couple of sips of wine, he hoped.

Suddenly there was a knock at the door. Well, all was prepared and Gethin W was ready for action. Unusual for Sally to come to the front door.

Then he remembered. In his paranoid state of mind, he'd locked all the doors to avoid any unwelcomed guests. This had to be his adorable bride of forty years ago wishing to come in. His heart was racing and he was high on the anticipation of his wife's reaction to his surprise. However, there was a sting in the tale.

He opened the door to greet his loving wife. What he hadn't anticipated was that her friend and partner in crime Gloria was also with her. His heart skipped a beat. His bubble had burst and he felt terribly deflated. This was going to be an interesting afternoon, he pondered.

Up until that moment everything was going to plan. He put on a brave face and his charm.

"Hello, my favourite ladies," he said jovially. Trying to uplift his own spirits.

"How are you, Gorgeous Gloria? Looking ravishing as usual," he said with a slight tone of sarcasm in his voice.

"Oh, Gethin Weedall, you've got that naughty glint in your eye again. What mischief have you been up to today?" she asked, giggling continuously.

Sally Anne on the other hand appeared cold and hostile. With an extremely stern expression on her face, she asked the obvious question. "What have you been up to today then? Bought any more thousands of bags of your *Devitas* online?" she asked with a razor-sharp tongue.

Oh dear. He'd almost been caught in the act. Trying to keep a cool head he had to think on his feet, and quickly.

He ignored the comment and just invited the ladies through to the lounge. He poured them a drink and closed the lounge door, allowing him a little breathing space to get his head together.

"Why did Grumpy Gloria have to come along and put a spanner in the works? It's so unfair," he said stamping his feet like a young boy who had just been reprimanded for being mischievous.

How can I get rid of her? he asked himself.

Off he went to get another chair from the garage and re-arrange the table settings. "Job done," he said, folding his arms and admiring his work of art, the fruits of his hard labour.

He made a quick change and he was ready for the enemy. As mentioned previously, Gloria and the professor were not exactly the best of friends. However, on this occasion he was going to be the perfect gentleman, the host with the most and try to treat her like a lady.

"How are you doing in here? Anyone for nibbles?" he asked in hope that these slightly inebriated women would bite his hand off.

"Oh, don't go to any trouble, Gethin. We've already had a snack in York. We'll stick to the liquid refreshment if it's all the same with you," replied Grumpy Gloria.

"Right. I'll just get the wine bottle. No! Change of plan. Why don't we go and sit in the garden? It's so sunny and warm," added the prof. He was determined to give them a sobering moment when presented with his special colourful mini buffet.

"That sounds good dear. We can sip our Italian and Spanish wine whilst watching you down on your hands and knees rooting out your weeds. Of course, we have wonderful scenery around here. So what a better place to be? Oh, what fun," Gloria screeched, slurring her speech not so slightly.

Sally Anne was on her own little mission to humiliate her husband and payback time was in order. So she wrongly assumed.

The man of the house was not amused, but he bit his tongue in the hope that he might just win back Sally's favour.

Okay. Here goes. The moment of truth, he thought. With Barry White playing gently in the background, and Champers chilled to perfection it was time to rock and roll. Fingers crossed. Hoping they'd appreciate his hard work and TLC.

You never know, perhaps even Grumpy Gloria might warm to me after she experiences my exquisite cuisine.

"Right then ladies shall we make a move?"

Sadly, all his hard work hadn't quite created the romantic ambiance he'd hoped for. But he was still going to make the most of it.

He wanted to tell his good lady all about the day's events, but it wasn't meant to be. Never mind. The afternoon was still early.

In hindsight, the prof didn't have to explain anything at all, as the reaction he received from both the ladies was without doubt, breathtaking. Far more than he could have expected.

The two women walked out on to the patio and were gobsmacked. Both a little tiddly, they stood near the table and examined the feast before them.

It was an OMG moment as Sally Anne was in a state of shock. She couldn't believe her eyes at what she was seeing. Tears welled up and she began to cry. Her husband was behaving like the charming, womanising, 007 hero figure he once was, whom she was so proud of. Then Grumpy Gloria started. The waterworks were flowing and the prof didn't know whether they were happy or sad.

"Is this to your satisfaction, ladies?" he asked nervously, not quite sure if it was the wine or that they genuinely appreciated this intimate banquet.

Both women looked at each other with sheer disbelief in their eyes.

"I can't believe it, darling. In all the years we have been together you've never done anything so romantic. Thank you. Come here and give me a big hug."

"Ooh, lovely, and one for me please," said Grumpy Gloria who was by now green with envy.

"Well, tuck in, please, ladies. I've been a tad busy today, as you can see. Can I just say this is my way of apologising for being such an utter pillock. I can assure you I won't be purchasing anything on the Internet in the future. I'll leave that to the younger generations. I've learnt my lesson the hard way and paid the price of almost losing the very special woman I love so dearly," he declared with passion.

Sally Anne and Gloria were in a state of shock, which was hardly surprising. Their eyes were literally popping out of their heads.

Outside the garage, to their amazement, there was nothing there. Sally Anne had to take two looks wondering if she'd had a little bit too much to drink at the wine bar in York, which she and Gloria undoubtedly had.

Her head was starting to spin. "Did you really do all this to say sorry?" she asked, disbelieving that her husband of over forty years, was capable of such a loving gesture.

"Of course, my dear. I hope you enjoy."

"So what happened to the weedkiller?"

"Well, that's a long story, which I'll share with you later," he smiled, half laughing, half crying.

Talking about crying. The flood gates were open and the ladies were blubbing away. Oh, it must be their hormones, he supposed. Probably rightly so.

Prof GW, the *King of Weeds* was now unofficially crowned the king of *nouvelle cuisine*.

"Right then, if you'll excuse me, I think I'll treat myself to a well-deserved beer or two. I'll be back in a mo. Please tuck in. There's plenty more where that came from," he told them.

As he opened up his chilled bottled beer, he was feeling highly delighted that he'd received the thumbs up from the ladies.

"I'm going to enjoy every sip of this," he told himself.

He looked longingly at the liquid refreshment, eager to taste and smell the hops. It was like nectar to the tongue as he munched on one of his delicious homemade mini quiches.

Oh, well done me. What an adventure. No one will ever believe my story but I know you will. You've been on this journey with me and it's not all over yet. The best was yet to come.

As he took another swig of beer, he heard the doorbell go.

Oh, no. Shall I answer it or not? I don't want to spoil our intimate dining experience. As Hyacinth Bucket (pronounced *Bouquet*) would undoubtedly say.

The bell kept ringing. Oh what shall I do? Well he didn't have much choice. I'll just have to answer, in frustration.

He opened the door to find no one there. How odd, he thought.

Then he realized what was going on.

Oh, no. This cannot be happening to me. What more surprises are in store? he asked himself. He was starting to feel helpless and losing control of the situation was beyond his comprehension.

He returned to the garden where he could clearly hear jovial voices. It wasn't Sally Anne or Grumpy Gloria, yet they did sound rather familiar.

The prof crept into the kitchen to have another glug of his fine beer before investigating what all the activity was.

With a huge sigh he prepared himself to face the music.

Oh yes. His worst nightmare. The entire neighbourhood, or it felt like it, had turned out to enjoy the celebration, including manager Mark and assistant Paul. But what celebration?

What am I going to do? he asked himself frantically trying to think ahead. Well, I'm going to have to make some sort of neighbourly speech, aren't I? I hate this sort of thing. I can see that everyone has very generously brought their own booze. So the least I can do is extend my hospitality.

"Come on darling, we have a few unexpected guests," his Sally Anne announced.

After another swig of beer for Dutch courage he stepped out not knowing what he was about to encounter. It's time to face the music. The show must go on.

"Hello, my friends. Thank you all for coming. I have to say this is somewhat of a surprise, but please feel free to enjoy our nibbles," he proudly announced, as his guests welcomed their host, applauding him with great vigour, though he didn't quite understand why. Just yet. "This has been a very memorable and most eventful day. One I will never forget, I can assure you," he declared, with a sigh of relief. This was time to let his greying hair down and unwind with his friends, family and neighbours.

Mrs Greengrass, the president of the Safer Homes committee put her hand up and explained why they had all turned up impromptu.

"Well, you see, Professor. I couldn't help noticing the comings and goings of those massive lorries recently. Well, when I realised, they were from the garden centre the pieces of the jigsaw puzzle started to come together. We all know about your situation and we are delighted that all is now in order. Let's all give a toast to our much-loved Professor Weed," she announced.

"Hear, hear," the rest of the neighbours voiced, in unison.

"On behalf of the neighbourhood Welfare Committee and all your friends and family we would like to thank you for your amazing achievements. We're so very proud of you and for rectifying a very difficult and embarrassing situation in such a small window of time. Also, we would like to present you with this plaque embellished in green as you would expect. It reads: This is where our famous *Serial Weed Killer of the North* lives."

Everybody applauded, enthusiastically and politely. And many, very many photos taken, both on camera and on mobile phones to capture this oddly memorable moment in time. Not to mention the local press attendance followed by vast amounts of TV coverage. After all, Prof Weedall was a star in his own right. A celebrity of sorts. Even if he didn't quite realise it.

Prof GW responded as best he could.

"Well, all I can say is, thank you all, from the bottom of my heart. Sally Anne and I are so fortunate to have such caring and generous neighbours and friends. It's so good to be back to the *Green, green grass of Home*, in the immortal words of fellow Welshman, Sir Thomas Jones. Thank you for your entertaining company this afternoon. It's certainly been a remarkable day to remember. Sally Anne and I would be delighted if you will all join us for our official garden party and the opening of our wonderful, well-tended garden area to the public. I'm starting to enjoy my new role as the host with the most," he added enthusiastically.

Sally Anne was in the background and laughing her pretty weed-embossed socks off, with good reason.

"Finally, I've just got one more, little announcement to make. This is to my gorgeous wife, Sally Anne," he said with pride, looking at her adoringly. "Now that we're finally back on track, I was wondering if you'd fancy a day or two somewhere a little different?" he asked her with confidence oozing from his slightly flushed face.

"Oh, yes, dear. That would be wonderful. It'd be good to have a change of scene. Just to be together again. Thank you so much my love."

"Well, I've done some research and I suggest visiting *The Secret Garden* in the South Wales Valleys, somewhere between Abergavenny and Pontypool. Perhaps we could stay overnight at a

Premier Inn and then stop off at Chepstow Garden centre on the way home," he said excitedly. "And pick up some more supplies of *Devitas*."

Well, you can imagine the reaction. Can't you? Not just from an enraged Sally Anne, but the entire neighbourhood. Everyone present gave a disapproving look and shook their heads in disbelief. With the mood changing, it became scary. The guests took long glugs of their drinks and not surprisingly the mayhem began.

It was fast becoming a lot like a sketch from an old Benny Hill comedy with Hill's Angels. Wow! Prof GW realised he had said the wrong thing — and made a run for it, to no avail. He was chased around his precious lawns by several of the disgruntled men and women armed with enormous pitch forks. Where did they come from? The forks. What a carry on.

Everyone was in high spirits, laughing about the farcical moments they'd previously experienced. All the neighbours left with full bellies. A few, well most, were a little bit worse for wear, but it was reassuring to know that in the main a good time was had by all.

Thank goodness that's all over. A small garden party to remember could have got out of hand and become a very ugly scene. Far from it. It didn't. Thankfully. What a wonderful day it had turned out to be, thought the Professor. Not all was lost, he added.

After a very eventful day and evening, Sally Anne and Gethin had a small nightcap before retiring to the comfort of their bed. Sally Anne took him by the hand and gently led him up the stairs and into her loving arms. It was worth everything to have him back.

Gethin came clean about his business transaction along with his experiences at the garden centre, not forgetting his new found friends, manager Mark and young Paul.

Once again, Sally Anne was in shock at her hero's behaviour and the drastic actions he'd taken to win her over.

"My darling. Thank you for everything. You have done so much for us all. I'll never forget this special time. There's just one last request I have before you embark on your massacre of the weeds tomorrow," she said. "You'll probably hate me for asking this, but is there any way we can keep a small patch of daisies, dandelions and forget-me-nots please?" she asked hoping he would melt at her request. Which he willingly did.

"Okay. Let's compromise my love. You know how hard I've worked to get to this milestone. However, I understand that your needs are just as important as mine," he beamed, glowing with affection. "How about I plant you your very own weed garden? We've got a few trellis pots in the garage and they would fit perfectly *in situ* on the patio. All I have to do is fill them up with compost and away you go." He looked into her bright eyes and kissed her gently on the cheek.

"That sounds brilliant. So we'll both get something positive out of this," Sally Anne said.

The couple cuddled up together, entwined lovingly once more in each other's arms, wrapped in a sense of ecstasy almost long-forgotten. Both enjoyed a very, very relaxing sleep, with a lot more of the affection previously shared.

While the prof's lawns had been his pride and joy, his paths and patio were equally important to him. Neatness and appearance were always the order of the day. Just like in that awful tawdry American series *Peyton Place*. To him, moss on the paths between paving stones and the brick-laid driveway also merited his regular attention. For that he had a special tool, a deadly tool, a weed paving brush gleaming with sloping metal bristles guaranteed to remove all stubborn weeds and moss with ease. And it did. But just in case, and to be on the safe side, he sprayed it all with, yes, *Devitas*.

And then summer came. A hot summer. A very dry, hot one. Rainfall was at an all-time low. Less than ten millimetres a month. Little really. The afternoon heat was blistering. The grass simply couldn't cope. Despite GW's daily watering with the hosepipe countless patches became bald, brown and threadbare. He was once again at his wits' end. His ever so beautiful lawns seemed to be dying in front of him, despite all his loving attention. He felt helpless, and no longer in control.

In desperation, he went back to his garden centre, and spoke to Paul, his now long-standing helpful assistant whom he trusted. Paul suggested a general-purpose fertiliser — and plenty of water. What else could he offer the frantic professor?

'This will do the trick,' he said confidently.

Somewhat reassured, he drove back to *his ranch* and straightaway diluted the fertiliser in his watering can as directed. The green can, of course.

With an element of pride, he slowly plodded up and down his beloved garden as he'd always done, spraying wildly in all directions, hoping to breathe new life into the grass he'd tenderly nurtured and cherished for so long.

And guess what? Yes, you can. Within a few days the green, ever luscious grass came back to life. And with a vigour. The blades grew, stronger than ever before, nourished by the vitalising phosphate fertiliser, refreshed from their silent slumber below ground. However, so too did the flaming **WEEDS**. Yes. **WEEDS**. Back to square one, if you understand.

Over the next few months, they shared quality time together in their garden. It gave the couple a new lease of life. A new dimension. And the beginning of a new chapter in their new book: *The Garden of Love*.

Yes, the couple had not only discovered their mutual interest in their lawns and weeds, they were also embarking on another joint venture, that of entering the literary world.

They'd been discussing their joy of reading and writing for some time. It all made perfect sense to combine their writing skills and share their unbelievable story with potential readers. All the humorous adventures, and the ups and downs they'd been on in order to rediscover each other and fall for one another all over again.

"It just goes to show that we can all change our lives around whatever our age," the prof said.

They both visited their second home on a regular basis, the wonderful garden centre, purchasing pot plant after pot plant, bird feeders and an atrium.

Soon the garden was alive with birdsong. They even had some nocturnal visitors. A family of hedgehogs could be heard noisily crunching away at the snail shells' sumptuous contents in the middle of the night. Sally Anne even put a saucer of milk out for them every evening, which they seemed to appreciate.

Sally Anne and the prof went on to spend many happy hours in their rickety rustic wooden sun house he'd cobbled together with its leaking roof at the bottom corner of their immense garden, watching all their animal friends feeding off the land. They reminisced about that day back in May and the *Devitas* challenge.

"This is our special haven and we've achieved it together. It's been a long and arduous journey, but we got there. We're a good team," the prof declared happily.

You could say the couple lived happily ever after, neither of them ever taking each other for granted again.

In a corny and ironic sort of way, there is no doubt that the saga of *Devitas* had played a big part in bringing the two lovebirds back together again.

Looking back, I wanted to destroy the weedkiller and eradicate it from our relationship, thought Sally Anne. However, they both knew *Devitas* was here to stay. Having fought for so long to be weed free she accepted that this chemical concoction had become a very important part of their lives.

Their lives had been transformed. Sally Anne and Prof Gethin David made a romantic date together once a week. Friday nights would never be the same again. They would become special, both would dress up for the occasion meeting up in a hotel bar pretending they were strangers. The new lovers to be.

Oh, how the romance had been rekindled and that long-lost special spark reignited, the passion returning into an almost forsaken lost marriage.

After all the excitement had died down and he'd spent a wonderful romantic and passionate night, several passionate nights, with his loving wife, he looked out of the window on a new dawn.

It was a gloriously sunny morning. Fluffy white clouds graced the azure sky, almost frolicking in heavenly repose. Back on Earth, Prof GW gazed out across his greenery. His wonderful, present world. And thoughts inexplicably came into his head. His past endeavours on behalf of Her Majesty's Government suddenly flooded his weary mind. Thoughts. Too many thoughts. His mind was awash with them Was he such a bad man? Why had he become an unscrupulous and uncaring killer of men? To order. That was it. To order. A trained killer without mercy? Showing no mercy whatsoever. With no feelings for his victims? Had it all been really necessary? All in the name of false political pursuits. What the bloody hell. Questions. Endless questions. With no sodding answers.

For now, in his mature years his conscience pricked him. Suddenly, he realised that after all he was human. With feelings. His wonderful, loving wife Sally Anne meant the world to him So why kill? Duty. And loyalty to the State. He wondered about that. He'd been callously used. Was it all really worth it?

And there was his family. And at what expense to his marriage and growing children? Yes, of course the money was important. Very important. He'd missed out on so much. He regretted missing out on his young girls growing up. He loved them to bits, as any caring father would. Yes, he'd spent many spells away from home. Out of necessity. Not choice. He'd sacrificed his family life for what? The dangerous world of untold adventures abroad in unsavoury places, the world of riff-raff, scum bags and drug traffickers. Again, he asked himself repeatedly, repeatedly, was it worth it?

Meanwhile, with an ironic change of conscience the seemingly uncaring professor looked at his lawns replete with the ever-persistent weeds, in a different light. A totally different light. After all, they were the strong ones. They were defiant. And suddenly, against everything he'd ever said, he admired them for that. The ageing, stubborn prof had food for thought. And reflection.

The weeds became his friends and he talked to them daily. His mental health became clearer. The anger, the frustration and bitterness he'd experienced during his working career began to evaporate. A sense of peace and calmness settled in his mind.

He realised how much he adored and cared for his loving wife. She had always supported him throughout his clandestine associations with the government agencies.

The local garden centre even had a special sign put up in pride of place next to the *Devitas* sign saying: 'Our best-selling weed-killing product. As endorsed by the renowned Professor Gethin David Weedall.' After all, *Devitas* was his saving grace.

What became of the weed killer saga and did the situation ever get resolved? Hmm. Watch this space if you have time to kill. *Weeds* and all.

What a dramatic climax to an amazing adventure of self-discovery.

Sally Anne and Gethin Spent a very romantic evening together once again. At last. For the first time in so many years they were back in each other's arms. Cuddling and kissing like they did back in the day when they were both innocent teenagers. This was the start of a new chapter in their lives and it was all down to that rickety old shed he had clumsily cobbled together. (So many years ago) Leaking roof was a serious problem. However, Prof W was too proud to ask for assistance from his good friends in the Greenalls Garden Centre.

Well, at the end of this story all I can say is that this shed became their summer house and a place of tranquillity and an opportunity for reminiscing about their wonderful married life they had shared together. Well, most of the time.

Having said that, now that prof was home and dry, he was becoming more and more sentimental and very loving towards his neglected wife.

With a bottle of the finest red wine and nibbles to match, they laugh, joked and relived the past. They talked about all the special moments they had spent together, reminiscing about so many events. So many happy moments never to fade away.

Sally Anne had admired and adored Gethin from the word go. It might sound a little bit cliché, but for Sally Anne it was literally love at first sight, if you know what I mean.

Mrs W was starting to become somewhat depressed with the whole weeding experience and it was taking its toll on her. Her GP advised her to seek some medical assistance from a psychologist.

She wasn't losing her mind. However, she was under pressure.

Having this romantic moment with Prof G, she was starting to see reality again and wake up and smell the coffee. (If that's the right expression).

Like any marriage, every day is so unpredictable. And, it's so true, when you take your vows you stick by them, through thick or thin.

The loving couple retired once more to their summer house and indulged in some more intimate moments.

What is more interesting is that Prof W made a very strong statement to his wife: "I hereby announce that our 'Weedall' will become the trophies within our summer house," he said with pride.

With that he ceremoniously placed all the remainder of the weedkiller on display within the home of their love shed.

Well, you have to admit, something good always comes out of something not quite so good.

So Mr and Mrs W enjoyed the peace and tranquillity of mature married life without WEEDS.

"Thank you *Devitas* for saving our marriage. You have been our saving grace," they both said as they cuddled up and rekindled their passions once again.

END OF THE SAGA OR IS IT? WATCH THIS SPACE FOR MORE.

ADDENDA
THE BACKGROUND BEHIND THIS HILLARIOUS TALE

I sincerely hope this foregoing story will resonate with my readers.

Hope you have enjoyed the story so far! There is much more to come.

To fully understand the personas and mindset of Professor Gethin David Weedall and his wife, Sally Anne, let us take a brief look at their respective backgrounds and upbringings.

Hopefully, this will lend credence to their escapades. For, despite all the odds, this seemingly mismatched couple adored each other totally. This would prove all the doubters wrong. They were totally devoted to one another and you could say *'Like two peas in a pod'*. Their successful marriage was based on trust, honesty, love and respect for one another.

So who were these eccentric characters they had become? And what influences in life had nurtured their personalities and interesting individualities?

Family members on both sides, of course. And the experiences of life. Just as you'd expect. Coming from two completely diverse backgrounds and despite all the odds, their relationship worked. Which is all that mattered, isn't it?

Gethin David Weedall was born in a snow-covered landscape on 18th February, 1951, along with his twin brother, Gareth Desmond. He was welcomed into a loving family along with two more older brothers. He was officially the youngest in the family.

Gethin and Gareth were born somewhat late in life to their mother, who was nearing her fifties. What an unexpected thrill. She adored them both completely from the start. But, unlike his fellow siblings, Gethin was unique in many ways. He was a red head, a ginger nut, a carrot top.

This was to become an initial problem for him. However, his RED HEAD turned out to be the making of him. Like most young people, his fellow friends would tease and taunt him about being a *'carrot top'*, at school, university and throughout adult life. Somehow, he seemed to find the strength to rise above it all and see the funny side of his brightly coloured mop. When I say RED, it most certainly was.

He eventually became proud of being officially a carrot top. He wore it like a badge with pride. Well, he did at one point consider dying it, but was put off when he thought about the consequences of turning black overnight. So there we are. "Carrot head I will remain and I am very proud of my roots," he told himself as he looked at his reflection in the mirror.

Not that it bothered him one iota. Why should it? But most importantly, Mum loved Gethin dearly. He was always there for her and there was a very special bond between them.

His father was a man who was still living within the regime of the military service. He'd done well for himself, a 'yes' man who had achieved the prestigious rank of colonel in the army's engineering corps. He knew how to build pontoon bridges over rivers and marshy ground across many Far Eastern war-torn territories; obviously of great importance in the theatre of war.

One questions whether or not his wife may have had a casual, or regular, romantic moments while her husband was away on duty. No one will ever know for sure.

However, there didn't seem to be an on-going love affair. But, at times, Mrs Margaret Weedall was so lonely.

The colonel had spent so much time away from home on missions, retaining deep and, dark secrets close to his chest. It wasn't an easy life. Basically, she was bringing up the family on her own.

Whilst he was away, she felt free and independent, becoming a bit of a socialite who enjoyed playing host to the supposedly wealthy upper crust of society. Inevitably she became one of them, wearing a false smile, pretending to enjoy their pretentious and over-bearing tawdry chatter and totally meaningless rubbish.

Most of them bragged about the number of lovers they had enjoyed, or supposedly so, over the years.

Mrs Weedall was devoted to her husband and proud of his career success and couldn't bear to think about being unfaithful to her loving husband. Well, only once?

She yearned for her husband so much and wondered if he would ever come home for good.

So, how did young Gethin fit into the equation? Well, when Dad occasionally came home, he didn't really have time for his son. He certainly didn't interact naturally as a proud father. He was always pre-occupied by his military experiences. It was as if he had been brainwashed into subservience, even after leaving the services to Her Majesty.

Yet Gethin heard, in his early teens, a casual chance remark about his looks that gave him food for thought. He, quite naturally, had always assumed Mum was his natural birth mother. But his instinct told him he had nothing in common with his brothers.

They were all very disciplined and abided by the household rules, dominated by their cantankerous father who had never shown Gethin any affection. This hurt him deeply as he never referred to him as Gethin. It was always just plain 'son'. Nothing else.

Just as if he was a thorn in the side of his perfect family. It was hardly a feeling of belonging, within a loving father-son relationship. The other brothers, ever-obedient and bereft of individuality, ever so quietly despised him. Why? Or did he just imagine it?

Just like his much older siblings, he was deliberately 'farmed out' at an early age to a renowned independent preparatory school for the *'sons of gentlemen'*. He hated every minute of it. The teachers were less than respectful and the cane worked overtime bringing supposedly unruly young boys to heel for the very slightest of misdemeanours.

But Gethin was alert, savvy and at a young age could see clearly through the protocol of this dictatorial institution. He realised how the status quo operated. 'Be a good boy and follow the rules.' That was the motto. The memories of his experience of prep school haunted him throughout his life. Break a lad's spirit and then you gained control over him for life.

Fortunately, at secondary school, his favourite old fuddy-duddy of a chemistry schoolmaster, Mr Hwyel Thomas, had a positive vision of Gethin and his potential. He encouraged him to believe in himself. He went on to excel in this chosen field, chemistry, and all the delights that came with it: blowing out the chem lab windows, filling the lab with smoke and setting fire mischievously to many fellow pupils' white coats.

You could say he was a potential time bomb. However, he was thoroughly enjoying himself. No intention of harming anyone. Chemistry lessons became crazy and a stage for utter entertainment.

Gethin was entranced with this new-found world of science. He wanted *'a slice of the cake'*, so to speak. He longed to be part of the science fraternity, to become a valuable member of it, which was clearly his destiny.

Despite the frowns and disapproving grimaces of his parents, he had finally discovered himself. He was now a new young man on a mission and had a unique personality that would eventually attract the love of his life.

He worked hard at his studies and, due to his dedication to science, was recognised as a star pupil. Being in receipt of an offer to continue his love of chemistry at Pembroke College, Oxford University, he eagerly grasped the opportunity with both hands.

Things were going his way and he felt proud of the fact that, despite all the bullying and ridicule he had endured over the years, he was going to make something of himself.

His new life was about to begin. And what exciting times lay ahead of him.

By contrast, Sally Anne had a completely different childhood and upbringing. Despite having a very domineering father who ruled her life, she became a kind and caring young woman who couldn't wait to escape the suffocating village in which she lived. She was an only child born to mature parents who were very protective of her. They had no high hopes for her educationally. In fact, they wanted her to marry a local farmer and spend her working life in the local supermarket.

She, though, had high hopes and expectations, and was determined to win the respect of her very conservative parents. The road ahead would prove to be a long one, but she would achieve her goals.

The youthful Sally Anne was full of life. A bundle of energy and a bit of a tomboy, you could say she had a slightly rebellious side to her personality. She was a square peg in a round hole, and so frustrated living within such a narrow-minded community.

Well, despite her parents' limited expectations for her future, she was on a mission to escape at the first chance.

She was fully aware that she was gradually being groomed by her hypocritical parents for a lifetime of servitude to the ministry of some omnipresent, mythical and benevolent God.

They wanted to control her and keep her close to home.

Her father, the Very Reverend Geraint Owain Davies, was a well-respected figure throughout the small-knit community of the picturesque fishing village of Aberpysgod ('above the fish') on the West Wales coastline of Cardigan Bay.

Interestingly, like Colonel Weedall, he too had many dark secrets; including, reputably, being an amorous ladies man.

Well, living within a small seaside village there was very little else to do other than gossip about everyone and everything, the rev always being the main talk of the community, for, no doubt, a variety of good reasons.

How his wife put up with it we shall never know. Mrs. Edna Davies played the perfect part as the vicar's wife. She was very popular throughout the village, always cheerful, and she happily enjoyed the company of the ladies in the women's circle.

It was all about flower arranging for forthcoming religious events, particularly wedding ceremonies. One asks how the good vicar could stand on his pulpit regularly preaching about commitment, loyalty and honesty to each other whilst he was playing away from home?

Well, despite his outwardly pious nature and ever-friendly smile, his daily ritual involved a daily cycle up the steep cobbled streets and pathways, his black cassock trailing wildly in the wind behind him, just like some bat out of hell, very reminiscent of that early American comic book and screen character, Batman, trying to put the world to rights, with hilarious consequences. But who now was the joker in the pack?

Naturally, this caused much laughter, amusement and derision in the local Port o' Call pub which he frequented every Friday and Saturday night. He was also a regular at the '*lock in*' for favoured patrons on a Saturday night. The seemingly righteous man of the cloth was equally fond of a pint or two or more of the finest ale on tap like his fellow parishioners. Rev Geraint heartily joined in the nightly banter and merriment which clearly earned him respect among fellow tipplers.

Or supposedly so. A true man of the people?

But his wife Edna was never there to support him. No. Her place was in the home, with their daughter, Sally Anne, just as Gethin's mother had been until his university days. However, this domesticity was the norm back in the day.

The rev was more than just a hypocrite with a very thick skin and few scruples. He regularly took his nightcap from the Holy Sacrament bottle of red wine. Or two. Talk about double standards.

He was known as the Vicar of Booze, aptly so, as he swayed around on his antiquated bicycle.

Sally Anne, in her tender teenage years, became increasingly uneasy with the rigidity of vicarage home life, especially on a Sunday, when it was compulsory to attend church *three* times.

Firstly, the early morning Eucharist (totally boring and meaningless which had to be endured), then afternoon Sunday school which was a little different. She thoroughly enjoyed being the Sunday school teacher, telling the young children all about the good deeds of Jesus, son of God, and his disciples.

Then there was the evening service attended by the self-righteous and pompous business people of the village in their Sunday best and hats. Most of the congregation frequented the local pub and '*lock in*'.

Sally Anne was a bright girl, and took everything in. You could say she was a very youthful Miss Marple; clever, with a very inquisitive mind. She could clearly see through the hypocrisy of this village life.

Sally Anne couldn't wait to escape from the straitjacket of life she found herself cocooned in at home.

So why did she put up with it? Simply because she enjoyed singing in the church choir. She had a sweet, lilting soprano voice which was growing stronger, more powerful with each passing year.

She was fast becoming the envy of the other choristers. An uplifting sense of freedom pervaded her whole being, a sense that she could express herself through the regular and monotonous rhythmic chants, hymns and the solo voice she was so blessed with. She was a born singer, with a natural talent, and content to sing solo in public at every opportunity. What pleasure that gave her.

Not forgetting her daily life at school, especially the local comprehensive school which was important to her. To mix with other boys and girls was good fun. Well, most of the time.

She was starting to mature through puberty, but still had very skinny legs, which the boys teased her about at the school gates with a chorus of *'chicken legs'* and *'cluck, cluck'*. Her breasts looked like fried eggs. Being of a sensitive nature she looked at her body every day in the shower and wondered.

The other girls in her year group were already well-formed, attractively so. Some were even far too top-heavy for their age, though that didn't stop them boasting about their breasts and the fact that they all had beautiful coloured lingerie. And all against the strict dictum of the school rules of navy blue. Small wonder the developing boys with rising testosterone levels were full of excitement, of awe, and enjoying *'hands on'* where possible.

But Sally Anne's bosoms were lying in wait. She hoped and prayed that they would grow and that one day she would be loved and appreciated by a gorgeous young man. She yearned to be the epitome of an ideal, desirable woman, full of self-confidence and passionate, which she would ultimately become.

She took the daily jibes at school all in good grace, normal day-to-day boy/girl banter. It didn't bother her one bit. Or did it? After all, at any age, we all have feelings of self-worth and self-respect, and have to live with whatever life unexpectedly throws at us.

She readily made friends, with one in particular becoming her best and trusted companion in class, one youthful and not too shy Gloria Honeydew. The pair of them always sat at the back of the class. No particular reason why, it just happened that way. And together they could be rather mischievous, taunting some of the more nervous and inexperienced young male teachers. Like Sally Anne, Gloria was the daughter of a member of the clergy, so they had much in common. He was a Methodist lay preacher with supposedly godly vows of self-righteousness and purity of spirit.

The two girls shared their innermost feelings and secrets together and had a special bond. It was such a release from the pressures of their teenage, hormonal years, even though they didn't quite realise it at the time.

Their favourite science teacher was a Dr Clive John Briggs, affectionately known as JCB. He had a certain way of captivating his subjects in more ways than other conventional teachers. They didn't have the same eccentric but lovable characteristics.

This elderly gentleman was different. He was of a nervous disposition. During lessons, his hands shook continuously. The worst time was when he was trying to explain *'the birds and bees'* to a somewhat rebellious class of fifteen-year-old pupils.

Led by Gloria's outspoken and cheeky questions, while giggling throughout, the class often reduced the poor chap to almost breaking point as his hands shook uncontrollably as he attempted to draw the over-sized male and pouting female genitalia on the blackboard. Most of the class thought it hilarious.

The more worldly-wise pupils were no strangers to this subject. Their carnal knowledge was probably far more advanced than their ageing teacher.

Not surprisingly, perhaps, being of dissimilar personalities, the two girls' academic pathways would take different but well-trodden routes. Gloria took the easier option, English, history and geography. Hardly so. But nevertheless, her chosen route to success.

Sally Anne, with a mind of her own, a steely determination and with a hatred of her suffocating religious upbringing, longed for the freedom and the power to express to the world her passion for science and it was to be chemistry. She worked hard at her A-levels. And guess what? Three As at chemistry, physics and pure and applied maths. She was overjoyed; so, too, her parents. With that qualification she was awarded a state scholarship to any university in England. She chose and was welcomed to Oxford, Pembroke College, in fact. Wow! And that was where she came across one 'carrot top', Doctor Gethin David Weedall, a research fellow of chemistry. The rest, as they say is history. As you've already found out. Happy days lay ahead.